Here is
a photo
of me

This Jacqueline Wilson
Address Book belongs to:

Name .....Lucy....Elizebeth.....
..................Vernon.......................

Address .....20 Dan-Yr-Heol......
...Cyncoed......Cardiff.............
..............CF23 6JU...................
....
....

Home phone number (029) ....
...............2075 6804..............

Mobile phone number ....
....

E-mail address ....
.....tutti.flutey@btintenet.......
...............com............................

Have you read all these wonderful
books by Jacqueline Wilson?

Published in Corgi Pups,
for beginner readers:

THE DINOSAUR'S PACKED LUNCH
THE MONSTER STORY-TELLER

Published in Young Corgi,
for newly confident readers:

LIZZIE ZIPMOUTH
SLEEPOVERS

Available from Doubleday/Corgi Books,
for older readers:

DUSTBIN BABY
GIRLS IN LOVE
GIRLS OUT LATE
GIRLS UNDER PRESSURE
GIRLS IN TEARS
LOVE LESSONS

The Jacqueline Wilson Address Book

Illustrated by Nick Sharratt

DOUBLEDAY

Join the FREE online

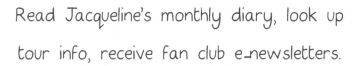

☆ FAN CLUB ☆

Read Jacqueline's monthly diary, look up

tour info, receive fan club e-newsletters.

All this and more, including members'

jokes and loads of exclusive top offers

Visit www.jacquelinewilson.co.uk

for more info!

Name

Addis, Sam, Paul, Scott, Dan

Address

Home phone number

Mobile phone number

E-mail address

Name

Address

Home phone number

Mobile phone number

E-mail address

Name

Address

Home phone number

Mobile phone number

E-mail address

Name

Address

Home phone number

Mobile phone number

E-mail address

Name

....

Address

....

....

....

....

Home phone number

....

Mobile phone number

....

E-mail address

....

Name

....

Address

....

....

....

....

Home phone number

....

Mobile phone number

....

E-mail address

....

Name

Address

Home phone number

Mobile phone number

E-mail address

Name

Address

Home phone number

Mobile phone number

E-mail address

Name

....

Address

....
....
....
....

Home phone number

....

Mobile phone number

....

E-mail address

....

Name

....

Address

....
....
....
....

Home phone number

....

Mobile phone number

....

E-mail address

....

Name

....

Address

....

....

....

....

Home phone number

....

Mobile phone number

....

E-mail address

....

Name

....

Address

....

....

....

Home phone number

....

Mobile phone number

....

E-mail address

....

Name

....

Address

....

....

....

....

Home phone number

....

Mobile phone number

....

E-mail address

....

Name

....

Address

....

....

....

....

Home phone number

....

Mobile phone number

....

E-mail address

....

Name

....

Address

....

....

....

....

Home phone number

....

Mobile phone number

....

E-mail address

....

Name

....

Address

....

....

....

....

Home phone number
                        /
....

Mobile phone number

....

E-mail address

....

Name

Address

Home phone number

Mobile phone number

E-mail address

Name

Address

Home phone number

Mobile phone number

E-mail address

Name

....

Address

....

....

....

Home phone number

....

Mobile phone number

....

E-mail address

....

Name

....

Address

....

....

....

Home phone number

....

Mobile phone number

....

E-mail address

....

Name

....

Address

....

....

....

....

Home phone number

....

Mobile phone number

....

E-mail address

....

Name

....

Address

....

....

....

....

Home phone number

....

Mobile phone number

....

E-mail address

....

Name

....

Address

....

....

....

....

Home phone number

....

Mobile phone number

....

E-mail address

....

Name

....

Address

....

....

....

....

Home phone number

....

Mobile phone number

....

E-mail address

....

Name

....

Address

....

....

....

Home phone number

....

Mobile phone number

....

E-mail address

....

Name

....

Address

....

....

....

Home phone number

....

Mobile phone number

....

E-mail address

....

Name

Address

Home phone number

Mobile phone number

E-mail address

Name

Address

Home phone number

Mobile phone number

E-mail address

Name

Address

Home phone number

Mobile phone number

E-mail address

Name

Address

Home phone number

Mobile phone number

E-mail address

Name

....

Address

....

....

....

....

Home phone number

....

Mobile phone number

....

E-mail address

....

Name

....

Address

....

....

....

Home phone number

....

Mobile phone number

....

E-mail address

....

Name

....

Address

....

....

....

....

Home phone number

....

Mobile phone number

....

E-mail address

....

Name

....

Address

....

....

....

....

Home phone number

....

Mobile phone number

....

E-mail address

....

Name

....

Address

....

....

....

Home phone number

....

Mobile phone number

....

E-mail address

....

Name

....

Address

....

....

....

Home phone number

....

Mobile phone number

....

E-mail address

....

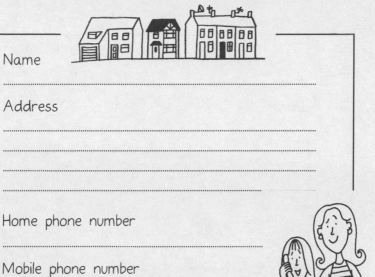

Name

....

Address

....

....

....

....

Home phone number

....

Mobile phone number

....

E-mail address

....

Name

....

Address

....

....

....

....

Home phone number

....

Mobile phone number

....

E-mail address

....

Name

....

Address

....

....

....

....

Home phone number

....

Mobile phone number

....

E-mail address

....

Name

....

Address

....

....

....

....

Home phone number

....

Mobile phone number

....

E-mail address

....

Name

....

Address

....

....

....

....

Home phone number

....

Mobile phone number

....

E-mail address

....

Name

....

Address

....

....

....

....

Home phone number

....

Mobile phone number

....

E-mail address

....

Name
....

Address
....
....
....
....

Home phone number
....

Mobile phone number
....

E-mail address
....

Name
....

Address
....
....
....
....

Home phone number
....

Mobile phone number
....

E-mail address
....

Name

....

Address

....
....
....
....

Home phone number

....

Mobile phone number

....

E-mail address

....

Name

....

Address

....
....
....
....

Home phone number

....

Mobile phone number

....

E-mail address

....

Name

Address

Home phone number

Mobile phone number

E-mail address

Name

Address

Home phone number

Mobile phone number

E-mail address

Name

Address

Home phone number

Mobile phone number

E-mail address

Name

Address

Home phone number

Mobile phone number

E-mail address

Name

....

Address

....

....

....

....

Home phone number

....

Mobile phone number

....

E-mail address

....

Name

....

Address

....

....

....

....

Home phone number

....

Mobile phone number

....

E-mail address

....

Name

....

Address

....

....

....

Home phone number

....

Mobile phone number

....

E-mail address

....

Name

....

Address

....

....

....

....

Home phone number

....

Mobile phone number

....

E-mail address

....

Name

....

Address

....

....

....

Home phone number

....

Mobile phone number

....

E-mail address

....

Name

....

Address

....

....

....

Home phone number

....

Mobile phone number

....

E-mail address

....

Name

....

Address

....

....

....

....

Home phone number

....

Mobile phone number

....

E-mail address

....

Name

....

Address

....

....

....

Home phone number

....

Mobile phone number

....

E-mail address

....

Name

....

Address

....

....

....

....

Home phone number

....

Mobile phone number

....

E-mail address

....

Name

....

Address

....

....

....

....

Home phone number

....

Mobile phone number

....

E-mail address

....

D

Name
....

Address
....
....
....
....

Home phone number
....

Mobile phone number
....

E-mail address
....

Name
....

Address
....
....
....
....

Home phone number
....

Mobile phone number
....

E-mail address
....

Name

Address

Home phone number

Mobile phone number

E-mail address

Name

Address

Home phone number

Mobile phone number

E-mail address

Name

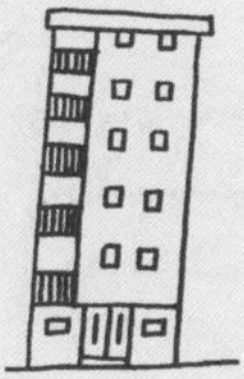

Address

Home phone number

Mobile phone number

E-mail address

Name

Address

Home phone number

Mobile phone number

E-mail address

Name

Address

Home phone number

Mobile phone number

E-mail address

Name

Address

Home phone number

Mobile phone number

E-mail address

Name

....

Address

....

....

....

....

Home phone number

....

Mobile phone number

....

E-mail address

....

Name

....

Address

....

....

....

....

Home phone number

....

Mobile phone number

....

E-mail address

....

Name

....

Address

....

....

....

....

Home phone number

....

Mobile phone number

....

E-mail address

....

Name

....

Address

....

....

....

Home phone number

....

Mobile phone number

....

E-mail address

....

Name

....

Address

....

....

....

....

Home phone number

....

Mobile phone number

....

E-mail address

....

Name

....

Address

....

....

....

Home phone number

....

Mobile phone number

....

E-mail address

....

Name

....

Address

....

....

....

....

Home phone number

....

Mobile phone number

....

E-mail address

....

Name

....

Address

....

....

....

....

Home phone number

....

Mobile phone number

....

E-mail address

....

Name

Address

Home phone number

Mobile phone number

E-mail address

Name

Address

Home phone number

Mobile phone number

E-mail address

Name

....

Address

....

....

....

Home phone number

....

Mobile phone number

....

E-mail address

....

Name

....

Address

....

....

....

Home phone number

....

Mobile phone number

....

E-mail address

....

Name

....

Address

....

....

....

....

Home phone number

....

Mobile phone number

....

E-mail address

....

E

Name

....

Address

....

....

....

....

Home phone number

....

Mobile phone number

....

E-mail address

....

Name

Address

Home phone number

Mobile phone number

E-mail address

Name

Address

Home phone number

Mobile phone number

E-mail address

Name

....

Address

....

....

....

....

Home phone number

....

Mobile phone number

....

E-mail address

....

Name

....

Address

....

....

....

....

Home phone number

....

Mobile phone number

....

E-mail address

....

Name

Address

Home phone number

Mobile phone number

E-mail address

Name

Address

Home phone number

Mobile phone number

E-mail address

Name

....

Address

....

....

....

....

Home phone number

....

Mobile phone number

....

E-mail address

....

Name

....

Address

....

....

....

....

Home phone number

....

Mobile phone number

....

E-mail address

....

Name

....

Address

....

....

....

....

Home phone number

....

Mobile phone number

....

E-mail address

....

Name

....

Address

....

....

....

....

Home phone number

....

Mobile phone number

....

E-mail address

....

Name

....

Address

....

....

....

....

Home phone number

....

Mobile phone number

....

E-mail address

....

Name

....

Address

....

....

....

....

Home phone number

....

Mobile phone number

....

E-mail address

....

Name

....

 Address

....

....

....

....

Home phone number

....

Mobile phone number

....

E-mail address

....

Name

....

Address

....

....

....

....

Home phone number

....

Mobile phone number

....

E-mail address

....

Name

....

Address

....

....

....

....

Home phone number

....

Mobile phone number

....

E-mail address

....

Name

....

Address

....

....

....

Home phone number

....

Mobile phone number

....

E-mail address

....

Name
Bethan + Rhiannon

Address
32 Dan-Yr-Heol
Cyncoed
Cardiff
~~South~~ glamorgan

Home phone number
~~20760800~~ 20763159

Mobile phone number

E-mail address Rhi- xxrhi-baybeexx @not.co.uk
Beth- earings_rock @hotmail.co.uk

Name
Kristin & Luke

Address
3 Burley Rd
Menston
West Yorkshire
LS29 6PG

Home phone number
01943 879 492

Mobile phone number
01972624780

E-mail address
tiger7217 @btinternet.com

Name
Rachel & Vicky

Address
30 Beresford Drive
WOODFORD GREEN
ESSEX
1G8 6JJ

Home phone number
02085046227

Mobile phone number Vicky- 07796187859O
Rach- 07790653657

E-mail address
vickyhourigan@hotmail.co.uk

F

Name
Lorna Egan

Address
Cloonlavish, Knock, COt
Mayo, Ireland
/Europer Earth
space

Home phone number

Mobile phone number

E-mail address

Name

....

Address

....

....

....

....

Home phone number

....

Mobile phone number

....

E-mail address

....

Name

....

Address

....

....

....

....

Home phone number

....

Mobile phone number

....

E-mail address

....

Name

....

Address

....

....

....

Home phone number

....

Mobile phone number

....

E-mail address

....

Name

....

Address

....

....

....

Home phone number

....

Mobile phone number

....

E-mail address

....

Name

Address

Home phone number

Mobile phone number

E-mail address

Name

Address

Home phone number

Mobile phone number

E-mail address

Name

....

Address

....
....
....
....

Home phone number

....

Mobile phone number

....

E-mail address

....

Name

....

Address

....
....
....
....

Home phone number

....

Mobile phone number

....

E-mail address

....

Name

....

Address

....

....

....

Home phone number

....

Mobile phone number

....

E-mail address

....

Name

....

Address

....

....

....

Home phone number

....

Mobile phone number

....

E-mail address

....

Name

....

Address

....

....

....

....

Home phone number

....

Mobile phone number

....

E-mail address

....

Name

....

Address

....

....

....

....

Home phone number

....

Mobile phone number

....

E-mail address

....

Name

....

Address

....

....

....

Home phone number

....

Mobile phone number

....

E-mail address

....

Name

....

Address

....

....

....

Home phone number

....

Mobile phone number

....

E-mail address

....

Name

....

Address

....

....

....

....

Home phone number

....

Mobile phone number

....

E-mail address

....

Name

....

Address

....

....

....

Home phone number

....

Mobile phone number

....

E-mail address

....

Name

....

Address

....

....

....

....

Home phone number

....

Mobile phone number

....

E-mail address

....

Name

....

Address

....

....

....

....

Home phone number

....

Mobile phone number

....

E-mail address

....

Name
....

Address
....
....
....
....

Home phone number
....

Mobile phone number
....

E-mail address
....

G

Name
....

Address
....
....
....
....

Home phone number
....

Mobile phone number
....

E-mail address
....

Name

Address

Home phone number

Mobile phone number

E-mail address

Name

Address

Home phone number

Mobile phone number

E-mail address

Name

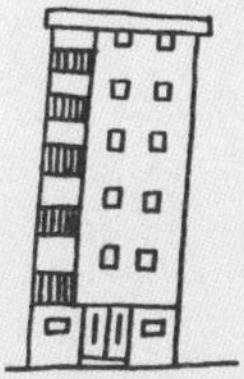

Address

Home phone number

Mobile phone number

E-mail address

Name

Address

Home phone number

Mobile phone number

E-mail address

Name

Address

Home phone number

Mobile phone number

E-mail address

Name

Address

Home phone number

Mobile phone number

E-mail address

Name

....

Address

....
....
....
....

Home phone number

....

Mobile phone number

....

E-mail address

....

Name

....

Address

....
....
....
....

Home phone number

....

Mobile phone number

....

E-mail address

....

Name

....

Address

....

....

....

Home phone number

....

Mobile phone number

....

E-mail address

....

Name

....

Address

....

....

....

Home phone number

....

Mobile phone number

....

E-mail address

....

Name

....

Address

....

....

....

....

Home phone number

....

Mobile phone number

....

E-mail address

....

Name

....

Address

....

....

....

....

Home phone number

....

Mobile phone number

....

E-mail address

....

Name

....

Address

....

....

....

....

Home phone number

....

Mobile phone number

....

E-mail address

....

Name

....

Address

....

....

....

....

Home phone number

....

Mobile phone number

....

E-mail address

....

Name

....

Address

....

....

....

....

Home phone number

....

Mobile phone number

....

E-mail address

....

Name

....

Address

....

....

....

....

Home phone number

....

Mobile phone number

....

E-mail address

....

Name

....

Address

....

....

....

....

Home phone number

....

Mobile phone number

....

E-mail address

....

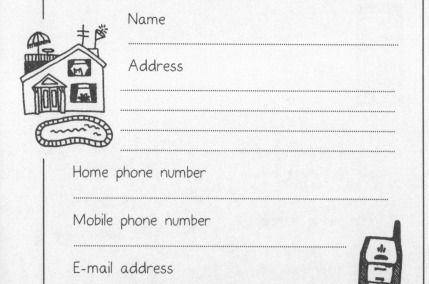

Name

....

Address

....

....

....

....

Home phone number

....

Mobile phone number

....

E-mail address

....

Name

....

Address

....
....
....
....

Home phone number

....

Mobile phone number

....

E-mail address

....

Name

....

Address

....
....
....
....

Home phone number

....

Mobile phone number

....

E-mail address

....

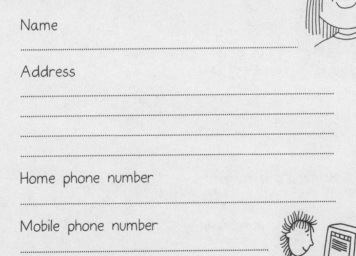

Name

....

Address

....

....

....

....

Home phone number

....

Mobile phone number

....

E-mail address

....

Name

....

Address

....

....

....

....

Home phone number

....

Mobile phone number

....

E-mail address

....

Name

....

Address

....

....

....

....

Home phone number

....

Mobile phone number

....

E-mail address

....

Name

....

Address

....

....

....

....

Home phone number

....

Mobile phone number

....

E-mail address

....

Name
....

Address
....

....

....

....

Home phone number
....

Mobile phone number
....

E-mail address
....

Name
....

Address
....

....

....

Home phone number
....

Mobile phone number
....

E-mail address
....

Name

....

Address

....

....

....

....

Home phone number

....

Mobile phone number

....

E-mail address

....

Name

....

Address

....

....

....

Home phone number

....

Mobile phone number

....

E-mail address

....

Name

Address

Home phone number

Mobile phone number

E-mail address

Name

Address

Home phone number

Mobile phone number

E-mail address

Name

....

Address

....

....

....

....

Home phone number

....

Mobile phone number

....

E-mail address

....

Name

....

Address

....

....

....

....

Home phone number

....

Mobile phone number

....

E-mail address

....

Name

....

Address

....

....

....

....

Home phone number

....

Mobile phone number

....

E-mail address

....

Name

....

Address

....

....

....

....

Home phone number

....

Mobile phone number

....

E-mail address

....

Name

Address

Home phone number

Mobile phone number

E-mail address

Name

Address

Home phone number

Mobile phone number

E-mail address

Name

....

Address

....

....

....

....

Home phone number

....

Mobile phone number

....

E-mail address

....

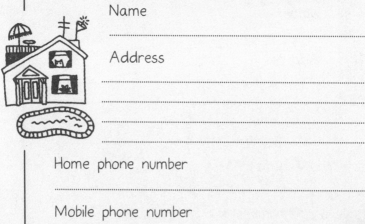

Name

....

Address

....

....

....

Home phone number

....

Mobile phone number

....

E-mail address

....

Name

....

Address

....

....

....

....

Home phone number

....

Mobile phone number

....

E-mail address

....

I

Name

....

Address

....

....

....

Home phone number

....

Mobile phone number

....

E-mail address

....

Name

....

Address

....
....
....
....

Home phone number

....

Mobile phone number

....

E-mail address

....

Name

....

Address

....
....
....
....

Home phone number

....

Mobile phone number

....

E-mail address

....

Name

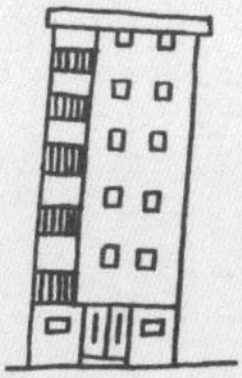

....

Address

....

....

....

....

Home phone number

....

Mobile phone number

....

E-mail address

....

Name

....

Address

....

....

....

....

Home phone number

....

Mobile phone number

....

E-mail address

....

Name

Address

Home phone number

Mobile phone number

E-mail address

Name

Address

Home phone number

Mobile phone number

E-mail address

Name

....

Address

....

....

....

....

Home phone number

....

Mobile phone number

....

E-mail address

....

Name

....

Address

....

....

....

....

Home phone number

....

Mobile phone number

....

E-mail address

....

Name

....

Address

....

....

....

....

Home phone number

....

Mobile phone number

....

E-mail address

....

Name

....

Address

....

....

....

Home phone number

....

Mobile phone number

....

E-mail address

....

Name
....

Address
....

....

....

Home phone number
....

Mobile phone number
....

E-mail address
....

Name
....

Address
....

....

....

Home phone number
....

Mobile phone number
....

E-mail address
....

Name

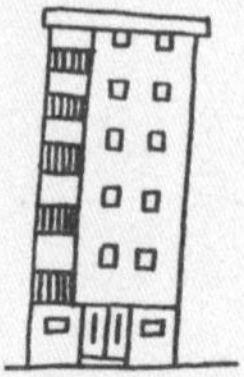

Address

Home phone number

Mobile phone number

E-mail address

Name

Address

Home phone number

Mobile phone number

E-mail address

Name

....

Address

....

....

....

....

Home phone number

....

Mobile phone number

....

E-mail address

....

Name

....

Address

....

....

....

Home phone number

....

Mobile phone number

....

E-mail address

....

Name

....

Address

....

....

....

....

Home phone number

....

Mobile phone number

....

E-mail address

....

Name

....

Address

....

....

....

....

Home phone number

....

Mobile phone number

....

E-mail address

....

Name

....

Address

....

....

....

....

Home phone number

....

Mobile phone number

....

E-mail address

....

J

Name

....

Address

....

....

....

Home phone number

....

Mobile phone number

....

E-mail address

....

Name

Address

Home phone number

Mobile phone number

E-mail address

Name

Address

Home phone number

Mobile phone number

E-mail address

Name

....

Address

....

....

....

....

Home phone number

....

Mobile phone number

....

E-mail address

....

Name

....

Address

....

....

....

....

Home phone number

....

Mobile phone number

....

E-mail address

....

Name

Address

Home phone number

Mobile phone number

E-mail address

Name

Address

Home phone number

Mobile phone number

E-mail address

Name
....

Address

....
....
....
....

Home phone number
....

Mobile phone number
....

E-mail address
....

Name
....

Address
....
....
....
....

Home phone number
....

Mobile phone number
....

E-mail address
....

Name

....

Address

....

....

....

....

Home phone number

....

Mobile phone number

....

E-mail address

....

Name

....

Address

....

....

....

Home phone number

....

Mobile phone number

....

E-mail address

....

Name

....

Address

....

....

....

....

Home phone number

....

Mobile phone number

....

E-mail address

....

Name

....

Address

....

....

....

....

Home phone number

....

Mobile phone number

....

E-mail address

....

Name

....

Address

....

....

....

....

Home phone number

....

Mobile phone number

....

E-mail address

....

Name

....

Address

....

....

....

....

Home phone number

....

Mobile phone number

....

E-mail address

....

Name

Address

Home phone number

Mobile phone number

E-mail address

Name

Address

Home phone number

Mobile phone number

E-mail address

Name

....

Address

....

....

....

....

Home phone number

....

Mobile phone number

....

E-mail address

....

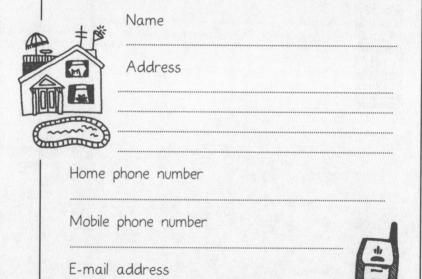

Name

....

Address

....

....

....

Home phone number

....

Mobile phone number

....

E-mail address

....

Name

....

Address

....

....

....

....

Home phone number

....

Mobile phone number

....

E-mail address

....

K

Name

....

Address

....

....

....

....

Home phone number

....

Mobile phone number

....

E-mail address

....

Name

....

Address

....

....

....

....

Home phone number

....

Mobile phone number

....

E-mail address

....

Name

....

Address

....

....

....

....

Home phone number

....

Mobile phone number

....

E-mail address

....

Name

....

Address

....

....

....

....

Home phone number

....

Mobile phone number

....

E-mail address

....

Name

....

Address

....

....

....

....

Home phone number

....

Mobile phone number

....

E-mail address

....

Name

Address

Home phone number

Mobile phone number

E-mail address

Name

Address

Home phone number

Mobile phone number

E-mail address

Name

....

Address

....

....

....

....

Home phone number

....

Mobile phone number

....

E-mail address

....

Name

....

Address

....

....

....

Home phone number

....

Mobile phone number

....

E-mail address

....

Name

....

Address

....

....

....

Home phone number

....

Mobile phone number

....

E-mail address

....

Name

....

Address

....

....

....

Home phone number

....

Mobile phone number

....

E-mail address

....

Name

....

Address

....

....

....

....

Home phone number

....

Mobile phone number

....

E-mail address

....

Name

....

Address

....

....

....

Home phone number

....

Mobile phone number

....

E-mail address

....

Name

....

Address

....

....

....

Home phone number

....

Mobile phone number

....

E-mail address

....

Name

....

Address

....

....

....

Home phone number

....

Mobile phone number

....

E-mail address

....

Name

Address

Home phone number

Mobile phone number

E-mail address

Name

Address

Home phone number

Mobile phone number

E-mail address

Name

....

Address

....

....

....

....

Home phone number

....

Mobile phone number

....

E-mail address

....

Name

....

Address

....

....

....

....

Home phone number

....

Mobile phone number

....

E-mail address

....

Name

....

Address

....

....

....

....

Home phone number

....

Mobile phone number

....

E-mail address

....

L

Name

....

Address

....

....

....

Home phone number

....

Mobile phone number

....

E-mail address

....

Name

....

Address

....

....

....

....

Home phone number

....

Mobile phone number

....

E-mail address

....

Name

....

Address

....

....

....

....

Home phone number

....

Mobile phone number

....

E-mail address

....

Name

....

Address

....

....

....

....

Home phone number

....

Mobile phone number

....

E-mail address

....

Name

....

Address

....

....

....

....

Home phone number

....

Mobile phone number

....

E-mail address

....

Name

....

Address

....

....

....

....

Home phone number

....

Mobile phone number

....

E-mail address

....

Name

....

Address

....

....

....

....

Home phone number

....

Mobile phone number

....

E-mail address

....

Name

....

Address

....

....

....

....

Home phone number

....

Mobile phone number

....

E-mail address

....

Name

....

Address

....

....

....

Home phone number

....

Mobile phone number

....

E-mail address

....

Name

....

Address

....

....

....

....

Home phone number

....

Mobile phone number

....

E-mail address

....

Name

....

Address

....

....

....

....

Home phone number

....

Mobile phone number

....

E-mail address

....

Name

....

Address

....

....

....

....

Home phone number

....

Mobile phone number

....

E-mail address

....

Name

....

Address

....

....

....

Home phone number

....

Mobile phone number

....

E-mail address

....

Name

....

Address

....
....
....

Home phone number

....

Mobile phone number

....

E-mail address

....

Name

....

Address

....
....
....

Home phone number

....

Mobile phone number

....

E-mail address

....

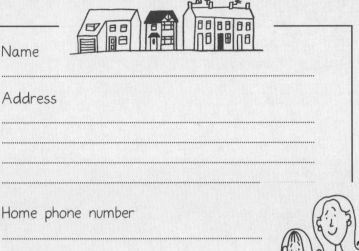

Name

....

Address

....

....

....

Home phone number

....

Mobile phone number

....

E-mail address

....

Name

....

Address

....

....

....

Home phone number

....

Mobile phone number

....

E-mail address

....

Name

....

Address

....

....

....

....

Home phone number

....

Mobile phone number

....

E-mail address

....

Name

....

Address

....

....

....

Home phone number

....

Mobile phone number

....

E-mail address

....

Name

Address

Home phone number

Mobile phone number

E-mail address

M

Name

Address

Home phone number

Mobile phone number

E-mail address

Name

Address

Home phone number

Mobile phone number

E-mail address

Name

Address

Home phone number

Mobile phone number

E-mail address

Name

....

Address

....

....

....

....

Home phone number

....

Mobile phone number

....

E-mail address

....

Name

....

Address

....

....

....

....

Home phone number

....

Mobile phone number

....

E-mail address

....

Name

....

Address

....

....

....

....

Home phone number

....

Mobile phone number

....

E-mail address

....

Name

....

Address

....

....

....

Home phone number

....

Mobile phone number

....

E-mail address

....

Name

....

Address

....

....

....

....

Home phone number

....

Mobile phone number

....

E-mail address

....

Name

....

Address

....

....

....

....

Home phone number

....

Mobile phone number

....

E-mail address

....

Name

....

Address

....

....

....

....

Home phone number

....

Mobile phone number

....

E-mail address

....

Name

....

Address

....

....

....

....

Home phone number

....

Mobile phone number

....

E-mail address

....

Name

....

Address

....

....

....

....

Home phone number

....

Mobile phone number

....

E-mail address

....

Name

....

Address

....

....

....

....

Home phone number

....

Mobile phone number

....

E-mail address

....

Name

....

Address

....

....

....

Home phone number

....

Mobile phone number

....

E-mail address

....

Name

....

Address

....

....

....

Home phone number

....

Mobile phone number

....

E-mail address

....

Name

....

Address

....

....

....

....

Home phone number

....

Mobile phone number

....

E-mail address

....

Name

....

Address

....

....

....

Home phone number

....

Mobile phone number

....

E-mail address

....

Name

....

Address

....

....

....

....

Home phone number

....

Mobile phone number

....

E-mail address

....

Name

....

Address

....

....

....

Home phone number

....

Mobile phone number

....

E-mail address

....

Name

....

Address

....

....

....

....

Home phone number

....

Mobile phone number

....

E-mail address

....

Name

....

Address

....

....

....

....

Home phone number

....

Mobile phone number

....

E-mail address

....

Name

....

Address

....

....

....

....

Home phone number

....

Mobile phone number

....

E-mail address

....

Name

....

Address

....

....

....

....

Home phone number

....

Mobile phone number

....

E-mail address

....

Name

....

Address

....

....

....

....

Home phone number

....

Mobile phone number

....

E-mail address

....

Name

....

Address

....

....

....

....

Home phone number

....

Mobile phone number

....

E-mail address

....

Name

....

Address

....

....

....

....

Home phone number

....

Mobile phone number

....

E-mail address

....

Name

....

Address

....

....

....

Home phone number

....

Mobile phone number

....

E-mail address

....

Name

Address

Home phone number

Mobile phone number

E-mail address

Name

Address

Home phone number

Mobile phone number

E-mail address

Name

....

Address

....

....

....

....

Home phone number

....

Mobile phone number

....

E-mail address

....

Name

....

Address

....

....

....

....

Home phone number

....

Mobile phone number

....

E-mail address

....

Name

....

Address

....

....

....

....

Home phone number

....

Mobile phone number

....

E-mail address

....

Name

....

Address

....

....

....

....

Home phone number

....

Mobile phone number

....

E-mail address

....

Name

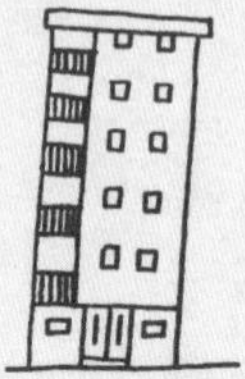

Address

Home phone number

Mobile phone number

E-mail address

Name

Address

Home phone number

Mobile phone number

E-mail address

Name

....

Address

....

....

....

Home phone number

....

Mobile phone number

....

E-mail address

....

Name

....

Address

....

....

....

Home phone number

....

Mobile phone number

....

E-mail address

....

Name

....

Address

....

....

....

....

Home phone number

....

Mobile phone number

....

E-mail address

....

Name

....

Address

....

....

....

....

Home phone number

....

Mobile phone number

....

E-mail address

....

Name

....

Address

....

....

....

....

Home phone number

....

Mobile phone number

....

E-mail address

....

Name

....

Address

....

....

....

....

Home phone number

....

Mobile phone number

....

E-mail address

....

Name

Address

Home phone number

Mobile phone number

E-mail address

Name

Address

Home phone number

Mobile phone number

E-mail address

Name

....

Address

....

....

....

Home phone number

....

Mobile phone number

....

E-mail address

....

Name

....

Address

....

....

....

....

Home phone number

....

Mobile phone number

....

E-mail address

....

Name

....

Address

....

....

....

....

Home phone number

....

Mobile phone number

....

E-mail address

....

Name

....

Address

....

....

....

Home phone number

....

Mobile phone number

....

E-mail address

....

Name

....

Address

....

....

....

....

Home phone number

....

Mobile phone number

....

E-mail address

....

Name

....

Address

....

....

....

....

Home phone number

....

Mobile phone number

....

E-mail address

....

Name

....

Address

....

....

....

....

Home phone number

....

Mobile phone number

....

E-mail address

....

Name

....

Address

....

....

....

....

Home phone number

....

Mobile phone number

....

E-mail address

....

Name

....

Address

....

....

....

....

Home phone number

....

Mobile phone number

....

E-mail address

....

Name

....

Address

....

....

....

Home phone number

....

Mobile phone number

....

E-mail address

....

Name

....

Address

....

....

....

....

Home phone number

....

Mobile phone number

....

E-mail address

....

Name

....

Address

....

....

....

....

Home phone number

....

Mobile phone number

....

E-mail address

....

Name

....

Address

....

....

....

....

Home phone number

....

Mobile phone number

....

E-mail address

....

Name

....

Address

....

....

....

Home phone number

....

Mobile phone number

....

E-mail address

....

Name
....

Address
....
....
....
....

Home phone number
....

Mobile phone number
....

E-mail address
....

Name
....

Address
....
....
....
....

Home phone number
....

Mobile phone number
....

E-mail address
....

Name

....

Address

....

....

....

....

Home phone number

....

Mobile phone number

....

E-mail address

....

Name

....

Address

....

....

....

....

Home phone number

....

Mobile phone number

....

E-mail address

....

P

Name

....

Address

....

....

....

....

Home phone number

....

Mobile phone number

....

E-mail address

....

Name

....

Address

....

....

....

....

Home phone number

....

Mobile phone number

....

E-mail address

....

Name

....

Address

....

....

....

Home phone number

....

Mobile phone number

....

E-mail address

....

Name

....

Address

....

....

....

....

Home phone number

....

Mobile phone number

....

E-mail address

....

Name

....

Address

....

....

....

Home phone number

....

Mobile phone number

....

E-mail address

....

Name

....

Address

....

....

....

Home phone number

....

Mobile phone number

....

E-mail address

....

Name

....

Address

....
....
....
....

Home phone number

....

Mobile phone number

....

E-mail address

....

Name

....

Address

....
....
....
....

Home phone number

....

Mobile phone number

....

E-mail address

....

Name

....

Address

....

....

....

....

Home phone number

....

Mobile phone number

....

E-mail address

....

Name

....

Address

....

....

....

Home phone number

....

Mobile phone number

....

E-mail address

....

Name

....

Address

....

....

....

....

Home phone number

....

Mobile phone number

....

E-mail address

....

Name

....

Address

....

....

....

Home phone number

....

Mobile phone number

....

E-mail address

....

Name

....

Address

....

....

....

....

Home phone number

....

Mobile phone number

....

E-mail address

....

Name

....

Address

....

....

....

....

Home phone number

....

Mobile phone number

....

E-mail address

....

Name

....

Address

....

....

....

....

Home phone number

....

Mobile phone number

....

E-mail address

....

Name

....

Address

....

....

....

Home phone number

....

Mobile phone number

....

E-mail address

....

Name

....

Address

....

....

....

....

Home phone number

....

Mobile phone number

....

E-mail address

....

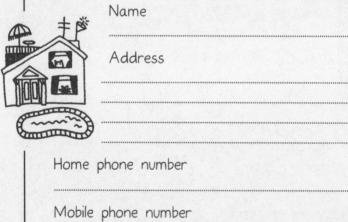

Name

....

Address

....

....

....

....

Home phone number

....

Mobile phone number

....

E-mail address

....

Name

....

Address

....

....

....

....

Home phone number

....

Mobile phone number

....

E-mail address

....

Name

....

Address

....

....

....

....

Home phone number

....

Mobile phone number

....

E-mail address

....

Q

Name

....

Address

....

....

....

....

Home phone number

....

Mobile phone number

....

E-mail address

....

Name

....

Address

....

....

....

....

Home phone number

....

Mobile phone number

....

E-mail address

....

Name

....

Address

....

....

....

Home phone number

....

Mobile phone number

....

E-mail address

....

Name

....

Address

....

....

....

Home phone number

....

Mobile phone number

....

E-mail address

....

Name
....

Address
....
....
....
....

Home phone number
....

Mobile phone number
....

E-mail address
....

Name
....

Address
....
....
....
....

Home phone number
....

Mobile phone number
....

E-mail address
....

Name

....

Address

....

....

....

....

Home phone number

....

Mobile phone number

....

E-mail address

....

Name

....

Address

....

....

....

....

Home phone number

....

Mobile phone number

....

E-mail address

....

Name

....

Address

....
....
....
....

Home phone number

....

Mobile phone number

....

E-mail address

....

Name

....

Address

....
....
....
....

Home phone number

....

Mobile phone number

....

E-mail address

....

Name

....

Address

....

....

....

Home phone number

....

Mobile phone number

....

E-mail address

....

Name

....

Address

....

....

....

....

Home phone number

....

Mobile phone number

....

E-mail address

....

Name

....

Address

....

....

....

....

Home phone number

....

Mobile phone number

....

E-mail address

....

Name

....

Address

....

....

....

....

Home phone number

....

Mobile phone number

....

E-mail address

....

Name

....

Address

....

....

....

....

Home phone number

....

Mobile phone number

....

E-mail address

....

Name

....

Address

....

....

....

Home phone number

....

Mobile phone number

....

E-mail address

....

Name

....

Address

....

....

....

....

Home phone number

....

Mobile phone number

....

E-mail address

....

Name

....

Address

....

....

....

....

Home phone number

....

Mobile phone number

....

E-mail address

....

Name
....

Address
....
....
....
....

Home phone number
....

Mobile phone number
....

E-mail address
....

Name
....

Address
....
....
....
....

Home phone number
....

Mobile phone number
....

E-mail address
....

R

Name

....

Address

....

....

....

....

Home phone number

....

Mobile phone number

....

E-mail address

....

Name

....

Address

....

....

....

....

Home phone number

....

Mobile phone number

....

E-mail address

....

Name

....

Address

....

....

....

....

Home phone number

....

Mobile phone number

....

E-mail address

....

Name

....

Address

....

....

....

....

Home phone number

....

Mobile phone number

....

E-mail address

....

Name

....

Address

....

....

....

....

Home phone number

....

Mobile phone number

....

E-mail address

....

Name

....

Address

....

....

....

Home phone number

....

Mobile phone number

....

E-mail address

....

Name

....

Address

....

....

....

....

Home phone number

....

Mobile phone number

....

E-mail address

....

Name

....

Address

....

....

....

....

Home phone number

....

Mobile phone number

....

E-mail address

....

Name

....

Address

....

....

....

....

Home phone number

....

Mobile phone number

....

E-mail address

....

Name

....

Address

....

....

....

Home phone number

....

Mobile phone number

....

E-mail address

....

Name

....

Address

....

....

....

....

Home phone number

....

Mobile phone number

....

E-mail address

....

Name

....

Address

....

....

....

Home phone number

....

Mobile phone number

....

E-mail address

....

Name

....

Address

....

....

....

Home phone number

....

Mobile phone number

....

E-mail address

....

Name

....

Address

....

....

....

....

Home phone number

....

Mobile phone number

....

E-mail address

....

Name

....

Address

....

....

....

....

Home phone number

....

Mobile phone number

....

E-mail address

....

Name

....

Address

....

....

....

....

Home phone number

....

Mobile phone number

....

E-mail address

....

Name

....

Address

....

....

....

Home phone number

....

Mobile phone number

....

E-mail address

....

Name

....

Address

....

....

....

....

Home phone number

....

Mobile phone number

....

E-mail address

....

Name

....

Address

....

....

....

....

Home phone number

....

Mobile phone number

....

E-mail address

....

Name

....

Address

....

....

....

....

Home phone number

....

Mobile phone number

E-mail address

....

5

Name

....

Address

....

....

....

....

Home phone number

....

Mobile phone number

....

E-mail address

....

Name

....

Address

....

....

....

....

Home phone number

....

Mobile phone number

....

E-mail address

....

Name

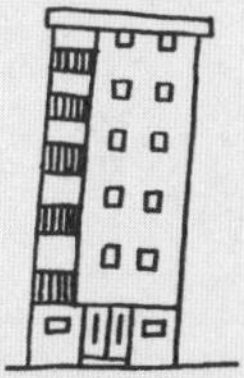

Address

Home phone number

Mobile phone number

E-mail address

Name

Address

Home phone number

Mobile phone number

E-mail address

Name

....

Address

....

....

....

....

Home phone number

....

Mobile phone number

....

E-mail address

....

Name

....

Address

....

....

....

Home phone number

....

Mobile phone number

....

E-mail address

....

Name

Address

Home phone number

Mobile phone number

E-mail address

Name

Address

Home phone number

Mobile phone number

E-mail address

Name

....

Address

....

....

....

....

Home phone number

....

Mobile phone number

....

E-mail address

....

Name

....

Address

....

....

....

....

Home phone number

....

Mobile phone number

....

E-mail address

....

Name

....

Address

....

....

....

....

Home phone number

....

Mobile phone number

....

E-mail address

....

Name

....

Address

....

....

....

....

Home phone number

....

Mobile phone number

....

E-mail address

....

Name

....

Address

....

....

....

Home phone number

....

Mobile phone number

....

E-mail address

....

Name

....

Address

....

....

....

Home phone number

....

Mobile phone number

....

E-mail address

....

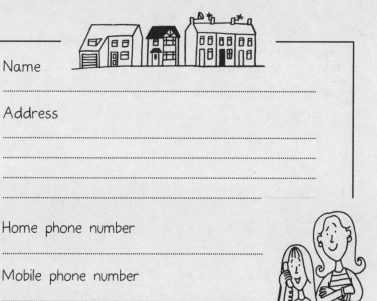

Name

....

Address

....

....

....

....

Home phone number

....

Mobile phone number

....

E-mail address

....

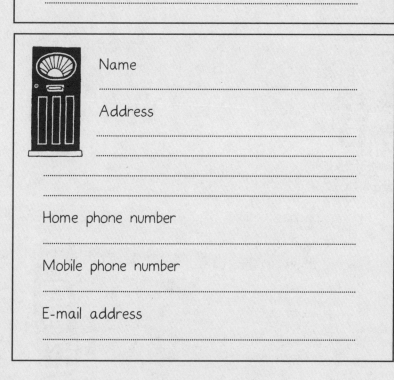

Name

....

Address

....

....

....

....

Home phone number

....

Mobile phone number

....

E-mail address

....

Name

....

Address

....

....

....

....

Home phone number

....

Mobile phone number

....

E-mail address

....

Name

....

Address

....

....

....

....

Home phone number

....

Mobile phone number

....

E-mail address

....

Name

....

Address

....

....

....

....

Home phone number

....

Mobile phone number

....

E-mail address

....

Name

....

Address

....

....

....

....

Home phone number

....

Mobile phone number

....

E-mail address

....

Name

Address

Home phone number

Mobile phone number

E-mail address

Name

Address

Home phone number

Mobile phone number

E-mail address

Name

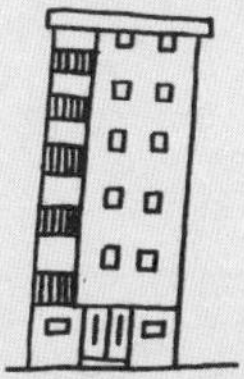

....

Address

....
....
....

Home phone number

....

Mobile phone number

....

E-mail address

....

Name

....

Address

....
....
....

Home phone number

....

Mobile phone number

....

E-mail address

....

Name

....

Address

....

....

....

....

Home phone number

....

Mobile phone number

....

E-mail address

....

Name

....

Address

....

....

....

....

Home phone number

....

Mobile phone number

....

E-mail address

....

Name

....

Address

....

....

....

....

Home phone number

....

Mobile phone number

....

E-mail address

....

Name

....

Address

....

....

....

....

Home phone number

....

Mobile phone number

....

E-mail address

....

Name

....

Address

....

....

....

....

Home phone number

....

Mobile phone number

....

E-mail address

....

Name

....

Address

....

....

....

Home phone number

....

Mobile phone number

....

E-mail address

....

Name

....

Address

....

....

....

....

Home phone number

....

Mobile phone number

....

E-mail address

....

Name

....

Address

....

....

....

....

Home phone number

....

Mobile phone number

....

E-mail address

....

Name

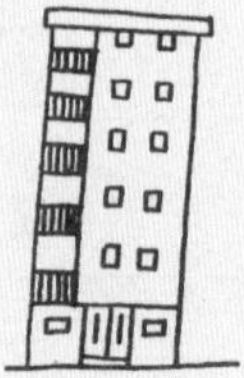

Address

Home phone number

Mobile phone number

E-mail address

Name

Address

Home phone number

Mobile phone number

E-mail address

Name

....

Address

....

....

....

....

Home phone number

....

Mobile phone number

....

E-mail address

....

Name

....

Address

....

....

....

....

Home phone number

....

Mobile phone number

....

E-mail address

....

Name

....

Address

....

....

....

....

Home phone number

....

Mobile phone number

....

E-mail address

....

Name

....

Address

....

....

....

....

Home phone number

....

Mobile phone number

....

E-mail address

....

Name

....

Address

....

....

....

....

Home phone number

....

Mobile phone number

....

E-mail address

....

Name

....

Address

....

....

....

....

Home phone number

....

Mobile phone number

....

E-mail address

....

UV

Name

Address

Home phone number

Mobile phone number

E-mail address

Name

Address

Home phone number

Mobile phone number

E-mail address

Name

....

Address

....

....

....

....

Home phone number

....

Mobile phone number

....

E-mail address

....

Name

....

Address

....

....

....

....

Home phone number

....

Mobile phone number

....

E-mail address

....

Name

....

Address

....

....

....

Home phone number

....

Mobile phone number

....

E-mail address

....

Name

....

Address

....

....

....

Home phone number

....

Mobile phone number

....

E-mail address

....

Name

....

Address

....

....

....

....

Home phone number

....

Mobile phone number

....

E-mail address

....

Name

....

Address

....

....

....

....

Home phone number

....

Mobile phone number

....

E-mail address

....

Name

....

Address

....

....

....

....

Home phone number

....

Mobile phone number

....

E-mail address

....

Name

....

Address

....

....

....

....

Home phone number

....

Mobile phone number

....

E-mail address

....

Name

....

Address

....

....

....

....

Home phone number

....

Mobile phone number

....

E-mail address

....

Name

....

Address

....

....

....

Home phone number

....

Mobile phone number

....

E-mail address

....

Name

....

Address

....

....

....

....

Home phone number

....

Mobile phone number

....

E-mail address

....

Name

....

Address

....

....

....

....

Home phone number

....

Mobile phone number

....

E-mail address

....

Name

....

Address

....

....

....

....

Home phone number

....

Mobile phone number

....

E-mail address

....

Name

....

Address

....

....

....

Home phone number

....

Mobile phone number

....

E-mail address

....

Name

....

Address

....

....

....

....

Home phone number

....

Mobile phone number

....

E-mail address

....

Name

....

Address

....

....

....

....

Home phone number

....

Mobile phone number

....

E-mail address

....

Name

....

Address

....

....

....

....

Home phone number

....

Mobile phone number

....

E-mail address

....

Name

....

Address

....

....

....

....

Home phone number

....

Mobile phone number

....

E-mail address

....

Name
....

Address
....
....
....
....

Home phone number
....

Mobile phone number
....

E-mail address
....

Name
....

Address
....
....
....
....

Home phone number
....

Mobile phone number
....

E-mail address
....

Name

....

Address

....

....

....

....

Home phone number

....

Mobile phone number

....

E-mail address

....

Name

....

Address

....

....

....

....

Home phone number

....

Mobile phone number

....

E-mail address

....

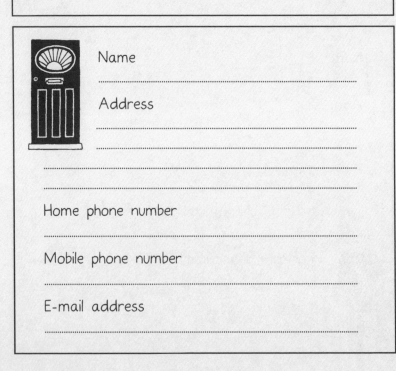

Name

....

Address

....

....

....

....

Home phone number

....

Mobile phone number

....

E-mail address

....

Name

....

Address

....

....

....

Home phone number

....

Mobile phone number

....

E-mail address

....

Name

....

Address

....

....

....

....

Home phone number

....

Mobile phone number

....

E-mail address

....

Name

....

Address

....

....

....

....

Home phone number

....

Mobile phone number

....

E-mail address

....

Name

....

Address

....

....

....

Home phone number

....

Mobile phone number

....

E-mail address

....

Name

....

Address

....

....

....

Home phone number

....

Mobile phone number

....

E-mail address

....

Name

....

Address

....

....

....

....

Home phone number

....

Mobile phone number

....

E-mail address

....

Name

....

Address

....

....

....

Home phone number

....

Mobile phone number

....

E-mail address

....

Name

....

Address

....

....

....

....

Home phone number

....

Mobile phone number

....

E-mail address

....

Name

....

Address

....

....

....

....

Home phone number

....

Mobile phone number

....

E-mail address

....

Name

....

Address

....

....

....

Home phone number

....

Mobile phone number

....

E-mail address

....

Name

....

Address

....

....

....

Home phone number

....

Mobile phone number

....

E-mail address

....

Name

....

Address

....

....

....

....

Home phone number

....

Mobile phone number

....

E-mail address

....

Name

....

Address

....

....

....

Home phone number

....

Mobile phone number

....

E-mail address

....

Name
....

Address
....
....
....
....

Home phone number
....

Mobile phone number
....

E-mail address
....

Name
....

Address
....
....
....
....

Home phone number
....

Mobile phone number
....

E-mail address
....

XYZ

Name

....

Address

....

....

....

....

Home phone number

....

Mobile phone number

....

E-mail address

....

Name

....

Address

....

....

....

....

Home phone number

....

Mobile phone number

....

E-mail address

....

Name

....

Address

....

....

....

....

Home phone number

....

Mobile phone number

....

E-mail address

....

Name

....

Address

....

....

....

Home phone number

....

Mobile phone number

....

E-mail address

....

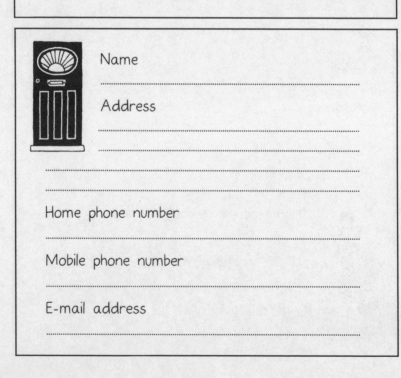

Name

....

Address

....

....

....

....

Home phone number

....

Mobile phone number

....

E-mail address

....

Name

....

Address

....

....

....

....

Home phone number

....

Mobile phone number

....

E-mail address

....

Name

....

Address

....

....

....

....

Home phone number

....

Mobile phone number

....

E-mail address

....

Name

....

Address

....

....

....

....

Home phone number

....

Mobile phone number

....

E-mail address

....

Name

....

Address

....

....

....

....

Home phone number

....

Mobile phone number

....

E-mail address

....

Name

....

Address

....

....

....

....

Home phone number

....

Mobile phone number

....

E-mail address

....

Name

....

Address

....

....

....

....

Home phone number

....

Mobile phone number

....

E-mail address

....

Name

....

Address

....

....

....

Home phone number

....

Mobile phone number

....

E-mail address

....

Name

....

Address

....

....

....

Home phone number

....

Mobile phone number

....

E-mail address

....

Name

....

Address

....

....

....

Home phone number

....

Mobile phone number

....

E-mail address

....

Name

....

Address

....

....

....

....

Home phone number

....

Mobile phone number

....

E-mail address

....

Name

....

Address

....

....

....

Home phone number

....

Mobile phone number

....

E-mail address

....

Name

....

Address

....

....

....

....

Home phone number

....

Mobile phone number

....

E-mail address

....

Name

....

Address

....

....

....

....

Home phone number

....

Mobile phone number

....

E-mail address

....

Name

_Zac_efron_offcial_fan_msn@hot.con_

Address

Home phone number

Mobile phone number

E-mail address

Name

Address

Home phone number

Mobile phone number

E-mail address

THE JACQUELINE WILSON ADDRESS BOOK
A DOUBLEDAY BOOK 978 0 385 61117 6 (from January 2007)
0 385 61117 X

Published in Great Britain by Doubleday,
an imprint of Random House Children's Books

First published in another format 2002
This edition published 2006

1 3 5 7 9 10 8 6 4 2

Set in Sharratt Medium

RANDOM HOUSE CHILDREN'S BOOKS
61–63 Uxbridge Road, London W5 5SA
A division of The Random House Group Ltd

RANDOM HOUSE AUSTRALIA (PTY) LTD
20 Alfred Street, Milsons Point, Sydney,
New South Wales 2061, Australia

RANDOM HOUSE NEW ZEALAND LTD
18 Poland Road, Glenfield, Auckland 10, New Zealand

RANDOM HOUSE (PTY) LTD
Isle of Houghton, Corner Boundary Road & Carse O'Gowrie,
Houghton 2198, South Africa

THE RANDOM HOUSE GROUP Limited Reg. No. 954009
www.**kids**at**randomhouse**.co.uk

A CIP catalogue record for this book is available from the British Library.

Printed and bound in China